The City Mouse and the Country Mouse

retold by Amy Helfer

illustrated by Loretta Krupinski

❧ A Classic Tale ❧

There was a city mouse. She went to visit her friend in the country.

City Mouse had never been to the country before. The grass was green, and the air smelled fresh.

"I think I will like the country," she thought.

Country Mouse served a fine meal. She thought the food was delicious.

But City Mouse did not agree. "Country food is different from city food," said City Mouse. "Come visit me in the city. You will love city food."

"I will visit you soon," said Country Mouse.
"But now it is late. Let me show you your
bed in the barn."

Country Mouse had made her friend a bed
in the hay, right next to her own. Country
Mouse thought the hay was warm and cozy.

But City Mouse did not agree. "This feels like pins and needles!" she thought. "How can anyone sleep in hay?"

"Come visit me in the city," said City Mouse. "You will love city beds."

"I will visit you soon," said Country Mouse. Then she yawned and fell asleep.

City Mouse could not sleep at all. The hay poked her and pinched her all night long. In the morning, City Mouse said good–bye and happily went back to the city.

The next month, Country Mouse visited her
friend in the city.

The buildings were tall, and the people were
busy. "I think I will like the city," thought
Country Mouse.

"Come in," said City Mouse. "But please
hurry! We have to run."

City Mouse and Country Mouse ran. Finally,
they stopped in a big room. City Mouse
waved her arm grandly. "Here we are!"
she said.

Country Mouse looked around her. She had
never seen so much food before.

"Have a taste of sugar," said City Mouse.

"Mmmm," said Country Mouse, licking her lips. "It is so sweet!"

"Try some butter," City Mouse said.

"OH!" said Country Mouse. "It is so delicious!" The little mouse ate and ate. She felt like the luckiest mouse in the world!

Just then, City Mouse squeaked, "Run!"

"What's wrong?" cried Country Mouse.

"The people are here!" yelled City Mouse.
"Run into that hole!"

The little mice ran as fast as they could
into a hole in the wall. Country Mouse was
shaking with fear.

"That was terrible!" said Country Mouse. "Does that happen all the time?"

"Oh," said City Mouse. "You get used to it after a while."

Country Mouse did not think that she could ever get used to it. City life was just too scary for her.

The mice sat inside the wall.

"We can have a nap here," said City Mouse.
"This is nicer than your scratchy old hay bed."

Country Mouse didn't agree. But, tired
from so much running, she closed her eyes
and slept.

When the mice woke up, it was quiet.

"Let's go back out!" said City Mouse.

In the kitchen, the mice saw big plates
of food everywhere.

Country Mouse sniffed and nibbled one
delicious dish after another.

Then Country Mouse saw a beautiful piece
of cheese in the corner.

"OH—I want some of that cheese!" Country
Mouse said.

"STOP!" cried City Mouse. "Don't eat it!
It's a terrible trap!"

Country Mouse stopped. "What's a trap?"
she asked.

"When you take the cheese, something comes
down on your head—**hard!**" said City Mouse.

14

Country Mouse jumped to the floor.

"I think I'll go home now, City Mouse," she said. "In the country, I never have to worry about traps coming down hard on my head! Good–bye!"

So Country Mouse went home.

She smelled the fresh air, she ate in peace,
and she slept in the warm, cozy hay. She was
happy to be a country mouse.

But she did dream about her visit to the city.
She dreamed about sugar, and butter . . .
and cheese.

The City Mouse and the Country Mouse

The Play

Characters

 Narrator 1

 Narrator 2

 City Mouse

 Country Mouse

Narrator 1

There was a city mouse. She went to visit her friend in the country.

Narrator 2

City Mouse had never been to the country before.

City Mouse

The grass is green, and the air smells fresh. I think I will like the country.

Narrator 1

Country Mouse served a fine meal. She thought the food was delicious. But City Mouse did not agree.

City Mouse

Country food is different from city food. Come visit me in the city. You will love city food.

Country Mouse

I will visit you soon. But now it is late. Let me show you your bed in the barn.

Narrator 2

Country Mouse had made her friend a bed in the hay, right next to her own. Country Mouse thought the hay was warm and cozy.

City Mouse

This feels like pins and needles! How can anyone sleep in hay? Come visit me in the city. You will love city beds.

Country Mouse

I will visit you soon.

Narrator 2

City Mouse could not sleep at all. The hay bed poked her and pinched her all night long. In the morning, City Mouse happily went back to the city.

Narrator 1

The next month, Country Mouse visited her friend in the city.

Country Mouse

Look at all these tall buildings and busy people. I think I will like the city.

City Mouse

Come in. But please hurry! We have to run.

Narrator 1

City Mouse and Country Mouse ran.

Narrator 2

Finally, they stopped in a big room.

City Mouse

Here we are!

Country Mouse

I have never seen so much food before!

City Mouse

Have a taste of sugar.

Country Mouse

Mmmm. It is so sweet!

 City Mouse

Try some butter.

 Country Mouse

OH! It is so delicious!

 City Mouse

Run!

 Country Mouse

What's wrong?

 City Mouse

The people are here! Run into that hole!

 Narrator 1

The little mice ran as fast as they could into a hole in the wall.

Narrator 2

Country Mouse was shaking with fear.

Country Mouse

That was terrible! Does that happen
all the time?

City Mouse

Oh, you get used to it after a while.

Narrator 1

Country Mouse did not think that she
could ever get used to it.

City Mouse

We can have a nap here. This is
nicer than your scratchy old hay bed.

Narrator 2

Country Mouse didn't agree. But,
tired from so much running, she
closed her eyes and slept.

Narrator 1

When the mice woke up, it was quiet.

City Mouse

Let's go back out!

Narrator 2

In the kitchen, the mice saw big plates of food everywhere. Country Mouse sniffed and nibbled one delicious dish after another.

Narrator 1

Then she saw a beautiful piece of cheese in the corner.

Country Mouse

OH—I want some of that cheese!

City Mouse

STOP! Don't eat it! It's a terrible trap!

Country Mouse

What's a trap?

City Mouse

When you take the cheese, something comes down on your head—**hard!**

Country Mouse

I think I'll go home now, City Mouse. In the country, I never have to worry about traps coming down hard on my head! Good–bye!

Narrator 2

So Country Mouse went home. She smelled the fresh air, she ate in peace, and she slept in the warm, cozy hay. She was happy to be a country mouse.

Narrator 1

But she did dream about her visit to the city. She dreamed about sugar, and butter . . . and cheese.